CW00820818

Explanatory Note: Rhodry is pronounced Rod-Ree

ACKNOWLEDGEMENTS

Thanks to Rachel for allowing us to use some of the pictures from when Rhodry was little. And for letting us take Druss and Rhodry home to join our family.

Also thanks to our friend Kay for all her help, advice and fun we have had with the hounds.

And of course, thanks to Gordon for arranging for Rhodry to join our family, and for tolerating the naughtiness once he'd arrived.

A Deerhound Called Rhodry

Deerhound Rhodry

Sophie Wallace

Copyright © 2016 Sophie Wallace and Deerhound Rhodry

First Edition

All rights reserved.

ISBN-13: 978-1540307378

ISBN-10: 1540307379

My name is Rhodry. This is my story from when I was a tiny puppy to when I went to live with my new family and all the adventures I had in my first year.

I was born just after Christmas. I had a brother and a sister. Our Mum is called Rona and we are Scottish Deerhounds. I am the one in the middle!

We all grew very quickly.
We opened our eyes when we were about two weeks old.
By the time we were three weeks old we were eating
our first proper food. I loved my food even then!

It wasn't long before we were big enough
to play properly and we had so much fun
playing tug of war!

Our Mum said soon we would choose our new families when they came to visit.

When we were six weeks old, a family came to see us. They had a Deerhound called Druss who needed a playmate. I knew this was the family for me.

I was as friendly as possible so my new family knew I had chosen them. I chewed the children's shoes to show how much I liked them. Mum says now she should have known back then....

In the same way that I knew instantly that this was the family for me, my new Mum knew I was the pup for her. It was love at first sight. I would go home with her in a few weeks.

Everyone was so happy to see me when we got home.
Druss seemed very big, and I felt very little, but he was friendly and showed me where everything was.

As well as Druss, there was another animal in the family. A big fluffy cat called Mushroom. Druss said I wasn't allowed to chase him. He was friendly, although he didn't want to play.

I was very tired after such an exciting
day so slept and slept and slept.

I loved collecting things and hiding them in my bed.

My favourite thing to collect was shoes. Especially Mum's shoes. She might not have minded so much if I hadn't chewed them quite so badly. Mum used to have lots of shoes

The other thing I liked to collect were the children's dolls. They used to have lots of dolls. They were sad when I chewed them, but Mum said I was doing something called "decluttering" and teaching them to put things away.

I loved the snow!
I could run very fast!

One day, I decided to
chew the beanbag to
see what was inside.

I chewed up Mum's favourite shoes.
And her second favourite shoes. And her wellies.
And all of the children's wellies.
And Mum's favourite hat.

One day I escaped.
I couldn't resist exploring
but went too far and got lost.
A kind lady found me and
took me to the Police Station
who got Mum to come
and get me.
I knew I was in Big Trouble
but Mum was so relieved I
was home safely she couldn't
stay cross with me for long.

Mum decided I should
go to something called Puppy Class.
I was nervous, but realised it was fun.
The other puppies were tiny compared to me, but we had a great time playing afterwards.

I loved to sit on the children's beds for bedtime stories.
Even though I wasn't allowed upstairs. And took up most of the bed.

One day we went to a Fun Dog Show. I met the tiniest dog I'd ever seen! His name was Spud and he was a chihuahua.

At the dog show, I did
my best trick and won my
class. And then I won
Best in Show!!

I loved our Christmas Tree with its sparkly decorations and twinkly lights. I only pulled it down once or twice trying to get a closer look.

I ate the sparkly Reindeer Food that Mum had made for Santa's Reindeer. Mum was cross with me, but couldn't stop laughing. I didn't understand why this was funny until later.
I ATE THE
GLITTERY REINDEER
FOOD AND I HAD
SPARKLY POO

I'm nearly as big as Druss now. We are best friends as well as brothers. I like knowing he is there to keep me company and play with.

By the time I was a year old, I was nearly as tall as Mum. She says I'm the naughtiest dog in the world but the best birthday present ever. I can't wait to have more adventures with my family.

ABOUT THE AUTHORS

Rhodry and his family live in Yorkshire, England. Rhodry's favourite pastimes are sleeping, eating, running and cuddles. And chewing things.

You can keep up with Rhodry's adventures on:
Twitter: @DeerhoundRhodry
Facebook: Rhodry the Scottish Deerhound

Sophie looks after Rhodry and the family and tries to stop Rhodry from chewing too many things she would like to keep.

Printed in Poland
by Amazon Fulfillment
Poland Sp. z o.o., Wrocław